BLEEDING FOR THE DEAD

VISHAL DIXIT

Made with ♥ on the Notion Press Platform
www.notionpress.com

Contents

Contents

Prologue

The journey began like any other. A familiar path, a comforting routine, a sense of predictability. My father, uncle, and I set out on a day that seemed ordinary, with no hint of the extraordinary events that would unfold. But life has a way of surprising us, of veering off course in unexpected ways.

As we walked, the landscape shifted, and the familiar gave way to the unknown. A flyover bridge in construction loomed before us, its pillars rising like skeletal fingers towards the sky. And then, I saw her. A girl, standing on one of the pillars, her gaze locked on mine.

In that moment, I felt a shiver run down my spine. A sense of unease settled over me, like a whispered warning. But I didn't listen. I couldn't look away.

And that's when everything changed.

Disclaimer

The events, characters, and settings depicted in this work are entirely fictional and not meant to be taken as representative of real-life events or individuals.

By reading this book, you acknowledge:

1. You understand this is a work of fiction intended for entertainment purposes only.

2. You release the author, publisher, and affiliates from liability for any emotional distress or discomfort.

READ AT YOUR OWN RISK

1

The Girl on the Bridge

As we walked, the hum of the city gave way to the rustling of leaves and the distant rumble of construction. My father, uncle, and I were on a mission to visit our relatives in a nearby town. The journey was familiar, one we had taken many times before. But today, something felt off.

The flyover bridge loomed before us, its pillars rising like giant sentinels. I had never seen it under construction before. The sight was both fascinating and unsettling.

And then, I saw her.

A girl, standing on one of the pillars, her gaze locked on mine. She wore a short pink Kurti, her dark hair blowing in the wind. But what struck me as odd was that my father and uncle seemed oblivious to her presence.

I was also surprised by the fact that she was standing on the pillar without any visible means of support. There were no stairs, no machines, no nothing. It was as if she had simply appeared there.

"Who's that girl?" I asked, my voice barely above a whisper, tugging on my father's sleeve.

He followed my gaze, his expression puzzled. "What girl, Vaasu? There's no one there."

I felt a shiver run down my spine. Why couldn't they see her? She was standing right there, her eyes fixed on mine with an unnerving intensity.

The girl's gaze never wavered, her eyes burning with an inner fire. I felt a sense of unease growing inside me, a feeling that something was about to go terribly wrong.

I stood there, frozen in confusion, as the girl's gaze seemed to bore into my soul. Her beauty was like nothing I had ever seen before – a radiant, ethereal quality that left me breathless. She was of average height, around 5'7", with a slim, delicate build that seemed almost fragile. Her open black hair cascaded down her back like a waterfall of night, framing her heart-shaped face and accentuating her striking features.

Her eyes, though, were what truly captivated me. They were an deep, piercing brown that seemed to see right through me, into the very depths of my soul. I felt a shiver run down my spine as she raised a hand, her fingers beckoning me towards her.

"Vaasu, come on!" my father called out, breaking the spell. "We need to keep moving."

But I couldn't tear my gaze away from the girl. She was mesmerizing, her presence both captivating and unsettling. I felt like I was drowning in her eyes, unable to look away even if I wanted to.

And then, just as suddenly as she appeared, she vanished.

The pillar was empty, the wind blowing through the empty space where she stood. I blinked, wondering if I had imagined the whole thing.

But deep down, I knew I hadn't.

2

The Encounter

I trailed behind my father and uncle, lost in thought as we walked along the deserted road. The trees seemed to close in around us, casting long, ominous shadows on the ground. Suddenly, I felt a chill run down my spine as a gentle touch grazed my shoulder.

I spun around, expecting it to be my father or uncle, but instead, I found myself face to face with the girl. Her eyes glowed with an otherworldly intensity, piercing through the darkness like lanterns in a graveyard.

Her touch sent shivers down my spine as she grasped my arm, her fingers like ice. I tried to speak, but my voice was frozen in my throat. My father and uncle were oblivious to the encounter, continuing their conversation as if nothing was amiss.

The girl's grip tightened, her eyes burning with an eerie light. I felt myself being drawn into their depths, unable to look away. It was as if she was pulling me into a nightmare from which I couldn't awaken.

And then, just as suddenly as she appeared, she vanished.

Leaving me shaken, confused, and wondering if I'd just imagined the whole terrifying encounter.

3

The Haunting

I couldn't shake off the feeling of unease that lingered long after the girl vanished. My father and uncle seemed oblivious to the encounter, but I knew what I saw. And I couldn't help but wonder if I was losing my mind.

As we continued our journey, the scenery around us grew more ominous. The trees seemed to twist and writhe, their branches like skeletal fingers reaching out to snatch us. The wind whispered eerie melodies, making my skin crawl.

I tried to focus on the road ahead, but my mind kept drifting back to the girl. Who was she? What did she want from me?

And then, I started seeing her everywhere. In the trees, in the shadows, even in the reflection of the windows. Her eyes seemed to follow me, haunting me with an unblinking gaze.

But it was her smile that really unnerved me. A faint, enigmatic smile that seemed to hint at secrets and mysteries beyond my comprehension. It was a smile that seemed to say, "I know something you don't."

I saw it in the trees, in the shadows, even in the reflection of the windows. Her smile seemed to be everywhere, haunting me with its eerie presence.

I knew I had to tell someone, but who would believe me? My father and uncle thought I was just tired, just stressed. But I knew the truth. I was being haunted.

By something. Or someone.

4

The Unrelenting Presence

I couldn't shake off the feeling of unease as I saw her everywhere on our journey. Her smile seemed to follow me, haunting me with its eerie presence.

I tried to focus on the road ahead, but her face kept appearing in my mind's eye. My father and uncle seemed oblivious to the strange occurrences, but I knew what I saw.

One moment, I was walking behind them, and the next, she was right beside me, her hand brushing against mine. I spun around, but she was gone.

I quickened my pace, trying to catch up to my father and uncle, but she appeared again, this time in front of me. Her smile grew wider, and I felt a chill run down my spine.

I tried to call out to my father, but my voice caught in my throat. She reached out and grabbed my hand from behind, pulling me off the path.

"Father!" I screamed, but my voice was drowned out by the rustling of leaves.

And then, she pulled me into the darkness, her smile the last thing I saw.

5

The Dark Journey

She pulled me through the darkness, her grip on my hand like a vice. We moved with a speed that felt like running, my feet barely touching the ground.

Suddenly, we stopped in an open ground, surrounded by nothing but emptiness. There was no one around, no trees, no buildings, just a vast expanse of nothingness.

I looked around frantically, but there was no escape. I was alone with her in this desolate place.

As I looked into her face, I realized with a jolt of terror that she was a ghost. Her eyes were black as coal, and her skin was deathly pale. The beauty that had caught my attention at first was still there, but it was now twisted into a grotesque mask. There was no beautiful expression on her face, only a cold, dead stare.

I tried to pull away, but she held me fast. I was trapped.

In desperation, I began to recite prayers, hoping to find some protection from the supernatural force that held me captive.

But she just laughed, a cold, mirthless sound that sent shivers down my spine. My prayers were useless in front of her, and she knew it.

And then, she slapped me, her hand cracking against my cheek with a loud thud. I felt a surge of pain and fear as I stumbled backward, my prayers dying on my lips

6

The Ghost's Wrath

I stumbled backward, my cheek burning from the slap. She advanced on me, her black eyes blazing with a fierce intensity.

"You think prayers can save you?" she hissed, her voice like a snake slithering through the grass. "You think you can escape me?"

I tried to speak, but my voice caught in my throat. I was paralyzed with fear, unable to move or speak.

She raised her hand again, and I flinched, expecting another blow. But instead, she touched my forehead, her fingers like ice.

"You will never leave this place," she whispered, her breath cold against my ear. "You will never escape me."

As she spoke, the world around me began to distort, like a reflection in rippling water. I felt myself being pulled into a dark vortex, unable to resist.

And then, everything went black.

She pulled me towards a water-filled structure, its depths dark and foreboding. I couldn't see the bottom, and the water's surface reflected the eerie atmosphere like a mirror.

As we reached the edge, she gave a sudden push, and I found myself tumbling forward, the water closing over my head like a shroud.

I tried to struggle, but she held me down, her grip like a vice. I was trapped, unable to escape.

The water was icy cold, and I could feel my lungs burning as I tried to hold my breath. But it was no use. She was too strong.

Just as I thought all was lost, she pulled me back up, my head breaking the surface with a gasp. I coughed up water, my eyes streaming with tears.

But she just laughed, her eyes gleaming with a malevolent light. "Not yet," she whispered. "You're not ready to die yet."

And with that, she pulled me back under, the water closing over my head like a coffin lid.

7

The Desperate Struggle

I kicked and struggled, but she held me down with ease. The water was suffocating me, and I knew I couldn't last much longer.

In a desperate bid to escape, I reached up and grabbed her hair, pulling with all my might. She screamed in rage, but didn't let go.

I pulled again, and this time, she stumbled backward, releasing her grip on me. I shot up out of the water, gasping for air.

But she was far from defeated. With a snarl, she launched herself at me, her hands grasping for my throat.

I dodged and weaved, avoiding her grasp, but she was relentless. We stumbled around the water-filled structure, crashing into the sides and sending water splashing everywhere.

I knew I couldn't keep this up for much longer. I needed a plan, and fast. Or else I'd be doomed.

With a surge of adrenaline, I overpowered the ghost, pinning her down beneath the water's surface. But as I looked into her eyes, I saw something that made my blood run cold.

She wasn't struggling. She wasn't even trying to escape. It was as if she had let me overpower her, as if she had wanted me to drown her all along.

I held her down, my heart racing with confusion and fear. Why would she want me to kill her? What was going on?

As the moments passed, her eyes seemed to bore into my soul, as if she was trying to communicate a message. And then, just as suddenly as it had begun, everything was over.

She went limp beneath me, her body sinking to the bottom of the water-filled structure. I pulled back, gasping for air, my mind reeling with questions.

But as I looked down at her still form, I saw something that made my heart skip a beat. A small, enigmatic smile played on her lips, as if she had finally found what she was looking for.

8

The Unexpected Twist

I overpowered the ghost, but my triumph was short-lived. She had let me win, and now she lay motionless, her body limp. The villagers gathered, their faces filled with horror and accusation. "Murderer!" someone shouted, and the police arrived, handcuffs at the ready.

But just as all hope seemed lost, the officers' expressions changed from suspicion to confusion. "Wait a minute," one of them said, "this is the same girl we found dead days ago, along with her parents." The ghost's plan was exposed, and she sprang back to life, her eyes blazing with fury.

She rampaged through the crowd, her ghostly powers causing chaos and destruction. I saw my chance to escape and took it, sprinting away from the mayhem. I jumped over a wall, landing hard on the ground, and kept running until I reached a nearby alleyway.

Breathless and shaken, I finally stopped to process what had happened. The ghost's plan had been foiled, but I knew she wouldn't give up easily. I had to find a way to protect myself from her next attack. But how do you stop a ghost who can manipulate the living?

As I looked around, I realized I was lost in an unfamiliar part of town. The alleyway was dimly lit, with buildings looming on either side. I had no idea where to go or what to do next. The ghost's enraged screams still echoed in my mind, and I knew I had to keep moving.

9

The Cursed Village and the Forest of Fangs

As I continued running, I found myself lost in an unknown place, unable to find my way back home. After several minutes of running, I stumbled upon a deserted village with no signs of life. The streets were empty, and the only indication of danger was the red skull symbol on the boards, warning of a cursed village. I felt like I had fallen from the sky and gotten stuck in a date tree.

My run eventually led me to a forest, where I encountered a cheetah charging towards me. I quickly climbed a tree, but soon found myself face to face with a lion and a tiger joining the cheetah. The lion and tiger goaded the cheetah into climbing the tree, planning to pull me down and devour me.

As the cheetah climbed, I grabbed a stick and used it to fend it off, but then a hidden man on the tree revealed himself, offering to help the predators in exchange for his own safety. I was more terrified of the man's selfish intentions than the cheetah's claws.

The man tried to make me fall, but I jumped from the top of the tree to another, like a monkey, shaking the entire tree and sending the cheetah and the man tumbling down. The three predators then turned on the man and ate him, leaving me shaken but alive.

I caught my breath and looked around, realizing that I was still lost in the forest. The trees seemed to close in around me, casting long, ominous shadows on the ground. I knew I had to keep moving, but my legs felt like lead and my heart was still racing from the encounter.

As I caught my breath and looked around, I realized that I was still being haunted by the ghosts. But these were no ordinary ghosts – they were skin walkers, able to take on the forms of predators. The cheetah, lion, and tiger that had attacked me were not animals at all, but malevolent spirits disguising themselves as beasts.

I remembered the words of an old wise woman I had met on my journey: "Beware the skin walkers, for they can take on many forms. They are the most cunning and dangerous of all the ghosts."

As I pondered the wise woman's words, I realized a crucial detail that further solidified my suspicion. The tiger, although menacing, was a creature of the forest, its natural habitat. However, the cheetah and lion were not native to this environment; they roamed the plains and grasslands, not the dense woods. This inconsistency only strengthened my conviction that they were not animals at all, but skin walkers in disguise.

Moreover, I noticed something even more unsettling. The three predators seemed to be communicating with each other, their eyes locked in a silent understanding. The cheetah nodded its head, the lion's tail twitched, and the tiger's ears perked up, as if they were conversing in a language beyond my comprehension. This unnatural behavior sent shivers down my spine, confirming my worst fears.

I knew I had to be cautious, for I was surrounded by malevolent entities that could take on various forms. The skin walkers' ability to blend in and manipulate their surroundings made them formidable foes. I had to stay alert, trust my instincts, and rely on my wits to survive this treacherous forest, where nothing was as it seemed.

It was a relief that they left after eating the man, I knew then that I had to be constantly on guard, for the skin walkers could appear at any moment, in any form. I couldn't trust my own eyes, for they could deceive me. I had to rely on my instincts, my intuition, to survive.

Paralyzed with fear, I remained perched in the tree, hiding from the sinister forces lurking below. I took a deep breath, trying to calm my racing heart, but my senses remained on high alert. From my perch, I scanned my surroundings with an intensity I never knew I possessed, searching for any sign of the skin walkers.

As I hid, the forest seemed to grow darker, the shadows deepening and twisting around me like living things. It was as if the very presence of the skin walkers was draining the light out of the world, leaving only an eerie, malevolent glow in its wake. The trees loomed above me, their branches like skeletal fingers reaching out to snatch me from above. I froze, holding my breath, as the darkness seemed to pulse with a life of its own. I knew I had to stay hidden, but the silence was oppressive, and I couldn't shake the feeling that I was being watched.

10

The Cursed Village's Dark Intentions

As I clung to the tree, a sense of foreboding settled over me like a shroud. The villagers gathered below, their voices dripping with malice, their eyes gleaming with a sinister intent. "Look, a new sacrifice for our cursed village," they cackled, their words sending shivers down my spine. "Let's catch him and lock him away, for the sake of our village."

Their words echoed through the deserted streets, a chilling reminder of the danger that lurked in every shadow. When the villagers tried to lock me away, I knew I had to act fast. My survival instincts kicked in, and I leapt from the tree to a nearby roof, my heart racing with fear.

I sprinted across the rooftops, the villagers hot on my heels, their footsteps pounding the tiles like a deadly drumbeat. The wind whipped through my hair, and my breath came in ragged gasps, but I didn't dare look back. I knew that if I fell, I'd be dragged back to the village, never to escape.

Just when I thought all was lost, I stumbled upon a group of cooks, gathered around a steaming cauldron, their faces lit by the flickering flames. I described my desperate situation to them, begging for their help, my voice shaking with fear.

"Please, you have to help me," I pleaded, my eyes scanning their faces for any sign of mercy. "They're trying to kidnap me, to sacrifice me for their cursed village. I don't know what they plan to do, but I know it can't be good."

The cooks exchanged nervous glances, their faces filled with a mix of fear and uncertainty. Would they help me, or would they turn me in to the villagers? My fate hung in the balance, as I waited for their response.

Their leader, a humble cook, stood tall, his worn cooking knife at the ready. Despite his ordinary profession, he possessed the heart of a legendary warrior and the kindness of a true hero. His eyes blazed with a fierce determination, and his voice thundered like a stormy tempest. "I dare you to touch the boy," he challenged the villagers, his tone firm and fearless. The ground seemed to tremble beneath their feet as he spoke, his words striking fear into the hearts of the evil villagers.

They realized that they would not be able to capture me without suffering heavy casualties, and their sinister plans began to unravel. The cook's bravery had turned the tables, and now they were the ones who were afraid. They turned and fled in disarray, abandoning their dark intentions.

I thanked the cooks, my voice filled with heartfelt gratitude. "Thank you for saving me," I said, my words barely above a whisper. "I owe you my life." I asked for directions, and they pointed me towards the path that would lead me home.

Finally, after what seemed like an eternity, I found my way back to the safety of my own city. But as I looked back at the cursed place, I knew that I had only scratched the surface of its dark secrets. The village still lingered, waiting for its next victim, its evil presence a constant threat. And I knew that I would never forget the terror I experienced within its borders, the memory of it etched into my soul like a scar.

11

The Return Home

I finally stepped through the front door, exhausted but relieved to be back in the familiar surroundings of my own home. The warm glow of the lamps, the comforting smell of fresh laundry, and the soft hum of the refrigerator all enveloped me in a sense of safety and normalcy. But as I walked further into the house, I was met with a mix of shock, tears, and joy.

My parents, who had been sitting in the living room, leapt to their feet, their faces etched with a mix of emotions. "Where have you been?" they asked in unison, their voices trembling with a blend of relief and concern. "You've been missing for a year!" they exclaimed, their words hanging in the air like a challenge.

I was taken aback, my mind reeling with confusion. "What do you mean?" I replied, my voice shaking slightly. "I was only gone for two days." I felt like I had stumbled into a parallel universe, where time had warped and twisted in ways I couldn't understand.

My parents exchanged a glance, their eyes filled with a deep sadness. My mother began to cry, her body shaking with sobs. "No, sweetie, you've been gone for a year," she said, her voice cracking with emotion. "We thought we'd lost you forever."

I felt like I had been punched in the gut, my breath knocked out of me. How could this be? I had only spent what felt like two days in the cursed village, trapped in a never-ending cycle of terror and fear. And yet, in the real world, a whole year had passed.

My mother hugged me tightly, tears streaming down her face. "We're just glad you're home safe," she said, her voice shaking with emotion. My father nodded, his eyes welling up with tears. "We reported you missing, and the police have been searching for you everywhere."

As we hugged, I felt a wave of emotion wash over me. I was overwhelmed with gratitude, relief, and a deep sense of wonder. Time had passed differently in the cursed village, warping and twisting in ways I couldn't understand. But I knew one thing for sure - I was home now, surrounded by love and safety. And I would never forget my terrifying experience in the cursed village.

12

Haunted by the Past

I lay in bed, staring at the ceiling as the darkness seemed to closing in around me. The girl's face lingered in my mind, her eyes piercing through the shadows. I couldn't shake off the feeling that she was still watching me, waiting for me to return to the cursed village.

Days passed, but the memory of the village and its inhabitants refused to fade. I felt like I was being pulled back, drawn into the heart of the curse. I tried to focus on my daily routine, but my mind wandered, reliving the terror I experienced.

One night, I woke up to the sound of whispers. Faint, but unmistakable. The words were indistinguishable, but the voice was hers. I sat up, my heart racing, and listened intently. The whispers grew louder, more urgent.

Suddenly, the room plunged into darkness. I was back in the cursed village, standing in front of the girl. She reached out a hand, beckoning me closer. I tried to step back, but my feet felt rooted to the spot.

The whispers stopped. The darkness receded. I was back in my bed, gasping for breath. But I knew then that I couldn't escape the curse. It had followed me home.

I knew I had to understand the curse if I wanted to break free from its grasp. I started researching, scouring books and online forums for any mention of skin walkers, cursed villages, or similar supernatural occurrences.

I spent long hours in the library, pouring over dusty tomes and ancient texts. I spoke to local experts, seeking out wisdom from those who claimed to know the secrets of the paranormal.

Slowly, a pattern emerged. The cursed village was just one of many, a nexus point for dark energies that crisscrossed the land. The skin walkers were mere symptoms of a deeper issue, a corruption that seeped into the fabric of reality.

I became obsessed with uncovering the source of the curse. I spent every waking moment studying, researching, and experimenting. My friends and family grew concerned, but I couldn't stop. I was driven by a singular focus: to break the curse and free myself from its grasp.

One night, while poring over an ancient text, I stumbled upon a passage that made my blood run cold. A ritual, hidden in plain sight, described a way to summon and control the skin walkers. But at a terrible cost...

13

The Weight of Knowledge

I felt like I was staring into the abyss, the words on the page searing themselves into my mind. The ritual promised power, control, and freedom from the curse. But at what cost? The text spoke of sacrifices, of innocent lives lost, of souls bound to the skinwalkers' will.

I couldn't shake the feeling that I was being tempted, that the curse was whispering sweet nothings in my ear. I thought of the girl, of the villagers, of the countless lives already lost to the darkness.

I began to question my own morality. Was I willing to pay the price for freedom? Could I live with the guilt of sacrificing others for my own salvation?

The more I grappled with the ritual, the more I felt myself slipping into the shadows. I became withdrawn, isolated, unable to share my burden with anyone.

One night, I caught a glimpse of myself in the mirror. The eyes staring back were no longer my own. They were haunted, sunken, and filled with a creeping darkness.

I realized then that I had a choice to make. I could succumb to the curse, embracing its power and sacrificing my soul. Or I could find another way, a path that wouldn't require me to become the very evil I sought to defeat.

I dived deeper and researched more about the cursed village then I found out about the dark past of the village.

The village's history was woven from threads of sorrow and despair. Founded by a tribe who sought refuge from a brutal war, it was meant to be a sanctuary. But the land itself seemed to be cursed, as if the earth remembered the bloodshed and suffering that had once occurred there.

As time passed, the villagers began to experience strange occurrences: crops withering, livestock falling ill, and people disappearing in the dead of night. They attributed it to the work of malevolent spirits, but the truth was far more sinister.

A powerful shaman, seeking to protect the village, made a pact with a dark entity from another realm. This entity granted the shaman immense power, but at a terrible cost: the village was bound to its will, forced to sacrifice its children to satiate the entity's hunger.

Generations passed, and the villagers forgot the truth, believing the sacrifices were necessary to appease their gods. But the entity's influence grew, corrupting the land and its people. The skinwalkers, once protectors of the village, became twisted servants of the entity, carrying out its dark bidding.

The girl I saw was a victim of this cycle, a sacrifice to the entity's eternal hunger. And I, by performing the ritual, had become a part of this tragic history, bound to the curse that haunted the village.

14

The Sinister Truth

I felt a chill run down my spine as I read the article. Aayu's name was etched in my mind, and her parents' brutal murder alongside her was a grim reminder of the village's dark secret.

The police had never caught the killers, and the case had gone cold. But I knew the truth. The villagers had taken them, using their supernatural connection to lure them to the cursed village. The ritual had been performed, and Aayu's spirit was trapped, forced to relive the horror of that night.

I couldn't shake the feeling that I was responsible, that my actions had awakened something that was meant to remain dormant. The ritual, the curse, the village – it all seemed to be connected to me now.

I began to experience strange visions, echoes of the past that seemed to sear themselves into my mind. I saw the villagers, their eyes black as coal, as they dragged Aayu and her parents to the altar. I saw the shaman, his eyes glowing with an otherworldly energy, as he performed the ritual.

And I saw Aayu, her eyes pleading for help, as she was consumed by the darkness.

I knew then that I had to make things right. I had to find a way to free Aayu's spirit, to break the curse that had haunted the village for so long.

But as I delved deeper into the mystery, I realized that I was not alone. There were others, watching me, waiting for me to uncover the truth.

I felt a sense of clarity wash over me as the pieces fell into place. Aayu's parents' souls were being held hostage, forcing her to do the villagers' bidding. They were using her as a lure, a bait to draw more people into the village for sacrifice. Her innocence and purity made her the perfect trap, and I had almost fallen into it myself.

But Aayu had tried to warn me, to frighten me away. She had seen something in me, a divine connection that gave her hope. She wanted me to help her, to free her parents' souls and break the curse that had consumed the village.

Yet, a nagging doubt crept into my mind. I had barely escaped the village last time, and only thanks to the bravery of the cook who had helped me flee. How could I possibly help Aayu myself? I was no match for the supernatural forces that controlled the village.

What if I was walking into a trap? What if I couldn't save Aayu or her parents? The thought sent a shiver down my spine, but I pushed it aside. I had to try. For Aayu, for her parents, and for the countless others who had fallen victim to the villagers' sinister plans.

With a deep breath, I steeled myself for the challenge ahead. I would need to gather allies, those who could help me navigate the supernatural forces at play. And I would need to confront the shaman, to put an end to the sacrifices and free Aayu and her parents from their torment.

As I prepared for the battle ahead, I felt Aayu's presence around me. She was watching me, waiting for me to make my move. I knew then that I was not alone in this fight. Aayu was with me, guiding me towards the truth and the freedom she so desperately sought.

15

Resolve

As I pondered the weight of my decision, I felt a surge of determination course through my veins. I knew I had to return to the cursed village, no matter the cost. The memory of Aayu's pleading eyes and the villagers' sinister intentions haunted me, fueling my resolve.

I thought of my family, and the long absence that lay ahead. But I knew I couldn't turn my back on Aayu and the others who suffered under the curse. I had been chosen to help, and I couldn't break the hope that had been placed in me.

With a sense of purpose, I began to make preparations for my journey. I knew it wouldn't be easy, but I was ready to face whatever lay ahead. As I packed my bags and bid farewell to my loved ones, I felt a sense of conviction that I had never felt before.

I was no longer just a curious traveler; I was a champion of hope, driven by a sense of responsibility to those who needed my help. And I knew that no matter what dangers or challenges awaited me, I would face them head-on, for the sake of those who had placed their trust in me.

Looking for the guidance I visited a very old yet not so famous temple, the Priest there was skinny and old but his face was full of light he was wearing many beads and was chanting Mantras with his eyes closed, with his closed eyes he sensed me coming and smiled.

The priest's smile was infectious, and I felt a sense of calm wash over me as I approached him. He opened his eyes, which sparkled with a deep wisdom, and motioned for me to sit beside him.

"Your path is fraught with danger, boy," he said, his voice low and soothing. "But I sense that you are driven by a noble purpose. You wish to free the village from the curse, and bring peace to the afflicted."

I was shocked that I haven't said a single word yet how he knows why I'm here still I nodded, feeling a sense of wonder at the priest's perceptiveness.

"I will give you what guidance I can," he continued. "But know that the journey ahead will test your courage, your wits, and your heart. You must be prepared to face your deepest fears, and to make sacrifices that will challenge your very soul."

The priest paused, studying me intently.

"But I sense that you are not one to shy away from a challenge. You have a fire within you, a flame of determination that will drive you forward even in the darkest of times."

He placed a hand on my shoulder, and I felt a surge of energy flow through me.

"Come," he said. "Let us begin your preparation. We have much work to do, and little time to waste."

16

A Legacy of Deceit

The priest's eyes seemed to gaze into the past, his voice filled with a mix of sadness and determination.

"My apprentice, the original shaman of the cursed village, was a good man," he said. "I taught him the ways of God's protection 210 years ago. He was eager to learn and help others, and I had hoped he would continue my work, keeping the village safe from harm."

The priest paused, his expression turning somber.

"But he grew old and passed away, leaving a power vacuum. The skin walker took advantage of his death, taking on his form and manipulating the villagers. It has been feeding on their souls and growing stronger with each passing year."

I felt a surge of anger at the skin walker's deceitful tactics.

"The skin walker has been masquerading as my apprentice for 150 years," the priest continued. "But I know the truth. And now, you know it too. You must stop the skin walker, no matter the cost."

I knew then that I had to stop the skin walker, no matter the cost.

The priest's words cut deep, revealing the sinister truth behind the villagers' actions.

"The villagers believe they are doing the gods' work," he said, "but in reality, they are mere pawns in the skin walker's game of power and control. They have been blinded by their devotion, misled into committing atrocities in the name of their faith."

I felt a surge of anger and sadness, knowing that the villagers were being manipulated and used.

"The skin walker has twisted their minds, feeding on their fear and ignorance," the priest continued. "It has become a master of deception, using their faith against them. But you, boy, have the power to stop this cycle of violence and free the villagers from its grasp."

He paused, his eyes gleaming with a knowing light.

"I see you've met her, Aayu. She will guide the way for you, lead you through the darkness and into the heart of the skin walker's lair. Trust in her, and trust in yourself. Together, you can break the curse and shatter the skin walker's hold on this village."

I nodded, feeling a sense of determination and purpose. I knew that I had to act, to follow Aayu's guidance and bring an end to the skin walker's reign of terror.

17

Armed for Battle

The priest placed a gentle hand on my shoulder, his eyes filled with a deep concern.

"Take this necklace, boy," he said, handing me a delicate chain with a small pendant. "It will protect you from the skin walker's manipulation, allowing you to see through his deceptions and illusions."

I took the necklace, feeling a surge of gratitude towards the priest.

"And this," he continued, handing me a small box of white

The priest's eyes seemed to gaze into the past, his voice filled with a mix of sadness and determination.

"My apprentice, the original shaman of the cursed village, was a good man," he said. "I taught him the ways of God's protection 210 years ago. He was eager to learn and help others, and I had hoped he would continue my work, keeping the village safe from harm."

The priest paused, his expression turning somber.

"But he grew old and passed away, leaving a power vacuum. The skin walker took advantage of his death, taking on his form and manipulating the villagers. It has been feeding on their souls and growing stronger with each passing year."

I felt a surge of anger at the skin walker's deceitful tactics.

"The skin walker has been masquerading as my apprentice for 150 years," the priest continued. "But I know the truth. And now, you know it too. You must stop the skin walker, no matter the cost."

I knew then that I had to stop the skin walker, no matter the cost.

The priest's words cut deep, revealing the sinister truth behind the villagers' actions.

"The villagers believe they are doing the gods' work," he said, "but in reality, they are mere pawns in the skin walker's game of power and control. They have been blinded by their devotion, misled into committing atrocities in the name of their faith."

I felt a surge of anger and sadness, knowing that the villagers were being manipulated and used.

"The skin walker has twisted their minds, feeding on their fear and ignorance," the priest continued. "It has become a master of deception, using their faith against them. But you, boy, have the power to stop this cycle of violence and free the villagers from its grasp."

He paused, his eyes gleaming with a knowing light.

"I see you've met her, Aayu. She will guide the way for you, lead you through the darkness and into the heart of the skin walker's lair. Trust in her, and trust in yourself. Together, you can break the curse and shatter the skin walker's hold on this village."

I nodded, feeling a sense of determination and purpose. I knew that I had to act, to follow Aayu's guidance and bring an end to the skin walker's reign of terror.

ash and an enchanted dagger. "Dip the dagger in the white ash and strike the skin walker on the head or neck. That will break the curse and free the village from his grasp, destroying the evil skin that holds his dark powers."

I felt a sense of determination and purpose, knowing that I had the tools to defeat the skin walker.

"The white ash is sacred," the priest explained. "It will weaken the skin walker's powers and make him vulnerable to attack. And the dagger... the dagger has been enchanted with the power of the gods. It is the only weapon that can pierce the skin walker's evil skin and shatter the curse."

I nodded, feeling a sense of resolve.

"I will do it," I said. "I will free the village and end the skin walker's reign of terror."

The priest smiled, his eyes filled with a sense of hope.

"I know you will, boy," he said. "You have the heart of a warrior and the spirit of a true hero."

As I turned to leave, the priest's last words echoed in my mind, reminding me of the brave cook who had helped me escape. I felt a surge of gratitude towards the priest and began to thank him, but he simply smiled and offered me his blessings.

"May the gods be with you, boy," he said. "May you succeed in your quest."

I nodded, feeling a sense of determination and purpose. But as I turned to leave, a thought suddenly struck me. How was the priest still alive after 210 years? I had been so caught up in the moment that I hadn't even considered it before.

I turned back to ask the priest, but he was nowhere to be found. I searched the temple, but there was no sign of him. I approached a young priest who was meditating in the corner and asked him about the old priest.

"Excuse me, young priest," I said. "I was just speaking with an old priest who looked like this..." I described the priest's appearance, and the young priest's eyes lit up with recognition.

"Ah, you mean our founding Guru?" he asked, pointing to a picture on the wall. The picture showed the old priest, surrounded by flowers and incense.

I nodded, feeling a sense of wonder. "Yes, that's him. But where is he now?"

The young priest chuckled. "He passed away over 150 years ago," he said. "He was a great spiritual leader and teacher. We still revere him as our founding Guru."

I was stunned. How could the priest have been alive and speaking with me just moments before? I felt a shiver run down my spine as I realized that I had been in the presence of something truly extraordinary.

18

The Journey Continues

I stood there for a moment, trying to process the revelation. But as I looked down at the dagger and necklace in my hands, I knew that I couldn't deny the encounter. I had truly met the priest, and he had given me the tools to defeat the skin walker.

Shaking off the confusion, I decided to continue my journey. I had a feeling that Aayu would meet me at the same pillar, but this time, our intentions would be different. I was no longer just a curious traveler; I was a warrior on a mission to break the curse.

As I walked, I felt a sense of determination and purpose. The necklace seemed to glow with an otherworldly energy, and the dagger felt heavy with power. I knew that I was ready to face whatever lay ahead.

After a few hours of walking, I saw the pillar in the distance. And as I approached, I saw Aayu waiting for me, her eyes shining with a fierce determination.

"You're back," she said, her voice low and husky. "I knew you would be."

I nodded, feeling a sense of camaraderie with this mysterious woman. "I'm here to break the curse," I said.

"Will you help me?"

Aayu smiled, a fierce glint in her eye. "I'll do more than that," she said. "I'll fight alongside you."

She paused, her expression softening. "I also wanted to apologize for last time," she said. "I didn't have a choice. My parents, and many other innocent souls, are being held captive by the skin walker. I had to protect them."

I nodded, understanding. "I know," I said. "I'm here to help you, and them."

Aayu's eyes flashed with gratitude. "Thank you," she said. "Together, we can defeat the skin walker and free our loved ones."

Aayu's expression turned serious, her eyes clouding over with concern. "The villagers will recognize you this time," she said. "No one has ever escaped them before, so they'll be on high alert. It'll be much harder for you to sneak in undetected."

I nodded, understanding the gravity of the situation.

"The help you got last time was a divine protection," Aayu continued. "It was the first time the cursed village's boundaries had come into contact with the real world, and the gods saw fit to intervene. But don't expect such luck this time. We'll need to be prepared for the worst."

I felt a shiver run down my spine as I realized the true extent of the danger we faced. But I was determined to press on, no matter the cost.

"What can we do to prepare?" I asked Aayu, my mind racing with strategies and plans.

Aayu smiled grimly. "We'll need to gather all the information we can about the skin walker's powers and weaknesses. And we'll need to come up with a solid plan of attack, one that takes into account the villagers' recognition of you and the lack of divine protection."

I nodded, my mind already racing with ideas. "Let's get to work," I said.

As we began to discuss our plan, I remembered the mysterious priest and the aid he had given me. "I forgot to tell you," I said to Aayu. "I met a priest who gave me a dagger and a necklace. He told me how to defeat the skin walker – I need to dip the dagger in white ash and strike the skin walker's head or neck. He also gave me a protective necklace that will prevent the skin walker's manipulation."

Aayu's eyes widened in surprise, but I could see the hope in her eyes. Maybe, just maybe, we had a chance to defeat the skin walker after all.

19

Gamble against Time

As I stood beside Aayu, preparing to face the skin walker once again, a sense of unease settled in the pit of my stomach. The weight of our mission hung heavy in the air, and I couldn't shake the feeling that we were running out of time.

"I'm just concerned about the time it'll take," I said to Aayu, my voice barely above a whisper. "Years might pass in the real world while I'm away."

Aayu's reassuring hand on my shoulder was a comforting presence, a reminder that I wasn't alone in this fight. "The village was once a part of the real world," she explained, her voice gentle but firm. "But as the skin walker's influence grew stronger, the village became disconnected from the real world, causing time to pass differently here."

I nodded, understanding the gravity of our situation. The skin walker's curse had created a rift between the village and the outside world, a rift that we had to bridge if we were to succeed.

"So, what happens if we defeat him?" I asked, my mind racing with the possibilities.

Aayu's smile was like a ray of sunshine, illuminating the darkness that surrounded us. "If we're successful, the curse will be lifted, and the village will rejoin the real world. Time will pass at the same rate as it does outside these boundaries. You won't lose years of your life this time."

As we talked, I felt a sense of camaraderie with Aayu, a bond that went beyond mere friendship. For a moment, I forgot that she was a ghost, a spirit trapped between worlds. Her presence felt so real, so solid, that I had to remind myself of her true nature.

I nodded, determination coursing through my veins like liquid fire. "Let's do this."

Aayu's smile faltered for a moment, and I saw a glimpse of sadness in her eyes. It was a reminder that she was not like me, that she was a ghost, a shadow of her former self. She could only guide and aid me, but she wouldn't be able to fight alongside me.

"I'm glad you're determined," she said, her voice barely above a whisper. "But remember, I'm not like you. I'm just a ghost."

I felt a pang of regret for forgetting her true nature, for expecting her to be something she's not. "I'm sorry, Aayu," I said, my voice filled with remorse. "I forgot. But your guidance and aid mean the world to me."

Aayu's smile returned, and she placed a spectral hand on my shoulder. "Let's go," she said, her voice firm and resolute. "We have a skin walker to defeat."

20

Planning the Assault

Aayu took my hand, her spectral touch sending a shiver down my spine. "Follow me, Vaasu," she said, leading me through the winding paths of the forest. "I know the way to the cursed village."

As we walked, the trees grew twisted and gnarled, their branches like grasping fingers. The air thickened with malevolent energy, and I could feel the skin walker's presence lurking just out of sight.

We reached the village, its buildings seeming to lean inwards, as if sharing a dark secret. Aayu's grip on my hand tightened, her eyes fixed on the path ahead.

"We need to come up with a solid plan to defeat the skin walker," I said, my voice barely above a whisper.

Aayu nodded, her ghostly form shimmering with determination. "We'll use the villagers' recognition to our advantage. If they know you, maybe we can use that to distract the skin walker or create an opening."

I considered her words, weighing the risks and benefits. "But what if the skin walker uses the villagers against us? We can't put them in harm's way."

Aayu's expression turned solemn. "We'll need to be careful, then. We can use the white ash to protect them, maybe create a barrier between them and the skin walker's influence."

I turned to Aayu, my mind racing with questions. "I need to find the shaman," I said. "But first, I want to tell you about the man I met by the tree."

Aayu's ghostly form leaned in, her eyes sparkling with curiosity. "What man?"

I recounted my encounter with the stranger, and Aayu listened intently. When I finished, she frowned. "That's strange. Skin walkers usually sacrifice their victims to gain power, not devour them." She added that I was the one who brought that man into the cursed village because the Skin Walker forced me to bring another sacrifice, but I asked him to hide on that tree so he could stay alive, I didn't knew that he was such a selfish man who would try to sacrifice you just to save himself. But it's still a strange that why did they devoured him.

"Exactly!" I said. "That's what I don't understand. Why did they eat him instead of sacrificing him?"

Aayu's expression turned thoughtful. "Maybe the skin walker is trying to absorb his essence, his life force. It could be a way to gain strength without alerting the villagers." Maybe the minions are trying to get stronger without getting noticed by the Shaman (Skin walker). After discussing for some time we decided to look for the Shaman's place.

I searched the village, Aayu by my side, until we found the shaman's hut, its wooden walls adorned with strange symbols and feathers. But as we approached, I felt a sense of unease, like a dark cloud was gathering above us. Something didn't feel right. Aayu seemed to sense it too, her ghostly form flickering with concern.

"Vaasu, I don't think this is a good idea," she whispered, her voice barely audible over the rustling of the wind.

I stood before the shaman's hut, Aayu by my side, my heart pounding in my chest. We both knew that the shaman was the leader of the skin walkers, and that he had been manipulating the villagers all along, using their fear and superstition to control them.

"Let's get this over with," I said, my hand closing around the holy pendant that hung from my neck. The pendant, imbued with the power of the gods, felt warm against my skin, a reminder of my mission to vanquish the forces of darkness.

Aayu nodded, her ghostly form shimmering with determination. "We need to put an end to his evil plans," she said, her voice firm.

We entered the hut, and the shaman looked up at us with a startled expression, his eyes widening in surprise. "Who are you?" he demanded, his voice harsh and menacing.

I held up the holy pendant, its light illuminating the dark recesses of the hut. "I am Vaasu, and I have come to put an end to your evil plans," I said, my voice firm.

The shaman's expression changed from surprise to anger, his eyes flashing with malevolence. "You dare to challenge me?" he snarled, his form beginning to shift and contort, his body stretching and twisting in ways that seemed impossible.

21

The Skin Walker's True Form

The shaman's eyes gleamed with malevolent intent as he began to weave his magic. His form started to shift and contort, taking on different shapes and appearances. One moment, he was a towering figure with glowing eyes, the next, he was a petite, innocent-looking girl who looked uncannily like Aayu.

"Vaasu, I'm the real Aayu," the girl-form said, her voice sweet and convincing. "Don't trust the ghost, she's trying to deceive you."

I hesitated, my mind clouded by doubt. But then, I remembered the pendant the priest had given me. I grasped it tightly, and suddenly, it began to glow with a soft, white light.

The light illuminated the shaman's true form, revealing the dark energy surrounding him. I saw through his deception, and my confidence returned.

"No, you're not Aayu," I said firmly. "You're the shaman, and you're trying to manipulate me."

The shaman snarled, his magic faltering as the pendant's light continued to shine. He attempted to transform again, but the light pierced through his illusions, revealing his true, monstrous form.

Ah, Vaasu, you think you're so clever, don't you? But you're no match for my power! I am the skin walker, and I have been manipulating the villagers by taking on the shaman's form!

But, I'll play along. Let the power of your precious pendant reveal my true form. Let it show you the horror that I am!

The pendant's light shines brighter, illuminating the skin walker's true form

Ah, yes! Look upon my true face, Vaasu! See the ugliness that lies beneath the surface! I am the one who has been manipulating the villagers, using the shaman's form to further my own dark agenda!

The skin walker's form contorts and twists, revealing a grotesque, inhuman visage

You may have the power of the pendant, but I have the power of the darkness! And with it, I will crush you!

22

The Minions Close In

The skin walker's scream echoed through the village, sending shivers down my spine. Aayu's ghostly form fluttered anxiously beside me as the villagers, still entranced, remained motionless, undisturbed by the commotion. They seemed to be in a deep sleep, oblivious to the danger lurking around them.

But I knew I was in grave danger. The skin walker's minions emerged from the shadows, their eyes fixed on me with an unnerving hunger. I was surrounded, outnumbered, and outmatched. The air was heavy with malevolent intent, and I could feel the weight of their gaze upon me.

I wasn't a subject of sacrifice to them anymore; I had become a threat, a obstacle to their dark plans. And they wanted to erase me as quickly as possible.

Aayu's voice whispered in my ear, "Vaasu, be careful! They won't hold back this time!"

I stood frozen, my heart racing, as the minions closed in. Their twisted faces seemed to blur together, a sea of snarling, snapping jaws and glowing eyes.

I knew I had to act fast, or I'd become their next victim. But what could I do against such overwhelming odds?

Aayu, being a spirit, couldn't help me physically, but she refused to leave my side. Instead, she subconsciously hid behind me, her fragile form trembling with fear. I knew I had to act fast to protect us both.

That's when I remembered the white ash box given to me by the priest. I quickly grabbed a handful of the ash and held it up, watching as the minions recoiled in terror. They knew they couldn't withstand the pain of the holy white ash.

The leader of the skin walkers, enraged by his minions' hesitation, attempted to throw the ash away from me. But I held firm, using all my strength to resist his supernatural force.

"Vaasu, be careful!" Aayu whispered, her voice trembling. "He's getting angrier!"

I gritted my teeth, determination coursing through my veins. I wouldn't let them win. I threw a pinch of the white ash at the leader, watching as he howled in agony, his dark form recoiling from the holy power.

The minions, emboldened by their leader's pain, began to close in once more. But I stood firm, ready to face them with the power of the white ash.

23

The Leader's True Power

The white ash had successfully repelled the minions, but I knew it wouldn't be enough to defeat the leader of the skin walkers. If it were, the priest would have never given me the holy dagger. The skin walker, confident in his own power, didn't know about the dagger, and I intended to keep it that way.

If he had known, he would have fled and hidden, trying to push me out of the cursed village. He would have seen me as a threat, and if that happened, I would never be able to return and save the villagers and captive souls. That's why I kept the dagger a secret, waiting for the right moment to strike.

The leader, enraged by his minions' defeat, began to transform into his true form. His body contorted and twisted, growing larger and more monstrous. His eyes glowed with an otherworldly energy, and I could feel his power growing.

Aayu, sensing my tension, whispered, "Vaasu, be careful! He's getting stronger!"

I gripped the dagger tightly, ready to face the leader's true power. I knew I had to time my attack perfectly, or risk being overwhelmed.

The skin walker's scream echoed through the village, "Choose the pain of holy ash or I'll kill you myself! I don't need cowards in my army!"

The minions, fearful of their leader's wrath, began to close in on me once more. I threw the holy ash at them, but they didn't stop. They burned, their bodies flailing in agony, yet they continued to attack.

Some of them managed to land a hit on me, their sharp claws tearing into my left arm. I felt a searing pain as blood began to pour out, soaking my sleeve.

The skin walker laughed, his voice dripping with ego, "This is the end of you, so-called hero!"

Aayu's voice trembled with tears and self-doubt, "Vaasu, I'm so sorry... I was so selfish, putting you in danger like that. I shouldn't have asked for your help. I'm the reason behind your suffering..."

She gazed at me, her eyes filled with anguish, "It's not worth it... you're **bleeding for the dead**. What's the point of saving souls that are already lost?"

Her words cut deep, and I felt a pang of doubt. Was I truly making a difference, or was I just throwing my life away?

24

The Pendant's Power Unleashed

As I struggled to keep my footing against the relentless minions, my breath grew shorter and my wound continued to bleed profusely. The flowing blood reached the pendant around my neck, but I didn't notice, too focused on the battle.

Suddenly, the pendant began to glow with an intense, blinding light. The minions let out a collective scream as they stumbled backward, covering their eyes. The light enveloped them, and they started to vanish, one by one.

The skin walker's eyes widened in shock as he realized what was happening to his minions. He stumbled backward, momentarily blinded by the light.

The pendant's glow began to fade, revealing only the skin walker standing before me. He looked around, confused and enraged, at the empty space where his minions once were.

Aayu's voice whispered in awe, "Vaasu, the pendant... it's responding to your selfless intent."

I stood panting, my wound still bleeding, but a sense of hope ignited within me. The pendant's power had given me a chance to turn the tide of the battle.

The skin walker snarled, baring his teeth, "You may have won this small victory, but I will still destroy you!"

The skin walker's enraged voice sent chills down our spines. "Your petty tricks won't defeat me! You're nothing more than a mere clown to me! And you, girl, you're the reason behind all this commotion. You brought that man here, hoping to defeat me and free your parents and other souls. I'll show you living hell once I'm done killing him!"

Aayu's grip on my back tightened, her fear palpable. But I felt a surge of responsibility to protect her, and my resolve hardened. I stood tall, eyes locked on the skin walker, and challenged him: "Bring it on! Let's settle this once and for all!"

The skin walker's eyes flashed with excitement, and he began to transform. His body grew larger, his limbs twisting and contorting in ways that seemed impossible. His skin turned a dark, mottled grey, and his eyes burned with an otherworldly energy.

Aayu remained silent, but the concern in her eyes for me was clear. I gave her assurance with a confident smile.

I nodded, my heart racing with anticipation. I knew this would be the final battle.

25

Reflections

As I gaze into Aayu's frightened eyes, I'm suddenly transported back to a time when I was powerless to save those I cared about. Memories I thought I'd long buried resurface, threatening to consume me.

I think about my past relationships, the ones I let slip away due to my inability to communicate. Friends drifted apart, and romantic interests grew tired of my silence. The weight of those losses slowly crushed my spirit, leaving me a shell of the person I once was.

But Aayu's presence in my life has awakened a spark within me, a desire to break free from the shackles of my past. I realize that my determination to save her isn't just about defeating the skin walker; it's about proving to myself that I'm capable of change.

With a newfound sense of resolve, I stand taller, despite the searing pain in my arm. I know I can't afford to hesitate, not now, not when Aayu's life hangs in the balance. The skin walker's taunts echo in my mind, but I silence them with a fierce determination.

"I won't lose anyone again," I whisper, the words barely audible. "I won't lose myself."

In this moment, I understand that my past doesn't define me. I have the power to rewrite my story, to become the person I'm meant to be. The question is, will I find the strength to see it through?

26

Reflections Shattered

As I stood there, lost in thought, the skin walker seized the opportunity to close in on me with his razor-sharp claws, intent on killing. My reflexes kicked in, and I swiftly pulled out the holy dagger, its blade shining with a faint, otherworldly glow. I had dipped it in white ash, awaiting the perfect moment to strike.

But the skin walker was no fool. He recognized the dagger, its history and power etched on his twisted face. He snarled, backing away, his voice dripping with malice. "Where did you find that dagger? I thought the priest was dead, taking his precious relic with him. Yet, here you are, wielding it against me."

His eyes narrowed, memories flashing across his face. "I thought I was finally free from the priest's meddling, but you've brought his legacy back to haunt me. Maybe I underestimated you... and the girl who brought you to my domain."

The skin walker's voice rose to a deafening scream, his fear and rage palpable. He knew that a precise strike from the holy dagger could end his existence, and he was determined to avoid that fate at all costs.

Despite the danger of death looming over him, the skin walker saw an opportunity to turn the tables. He seized on my weakened state, relishing in my misery. I had been bleeding for far too long, and my vision began to blur. My breaths came in ragged gasps, and I could barely keep myself standing, let alone hold onto the dagger.

The skin walker's laughter cut through the air, a cold, mirthless sound. "Boy, you should've stayed home when you once escaped me. But maybe you're just too unlucky, walking right into the mouth of death yourself." He sneered, his words dripping with contempt. "I pity you, boy. I'll end your suffering now."

With a flourish, the skin walker began to toy with me, attacking from different angles, his claws raking across my skin with precision. Thin wounds opened up on my chest, back, hands, and legs, each one stinging like a hot brand. I stumbled, my body screaming in agony as I bled profusely.

The skin walker reveled in my suffering, his eyes gleaming with sadistic pleasure. I knew I couldn't keep this up for much longer. My strength was waning, and my vision began to fade. The dagger, once a symbol of hope, now felt like a dead weight in my hand. I was running out of time...

27

The Final Confrontation

The skin walker's words dripped with condescension, his ego bloated like a festering wound. "You might have acquired the holy dagger and white ash, my weaknesses, but you're no match for me. I feared the priest, and you think you can defeat me? Don't try to mimic the superhumans, you're nothing more than a mere clown."

He attacked, his claws flashing In the dim light, cutting the pendant chain and sending it crashing to the ground. But I had planned this, feigning weakness to lull him into a false sense of security. The skin walker didn't realize that I had been playing a careful game, using my brains to outmaneuver him.

"I waited until the priest died, and now you think you can take his place?" He sneered, his voice dripping with disdain. "You're no substitute for the real thing. Your attempts to mimic him are pathetic."

His words struck a chord, but I knew I couldn't let him get inside my head. I had something he didn't: cunning and determination. I would use every trick in the book to bring him down.

With a fierce cry, I launched myself at the skin walker, the holy dagger flashing in my hand. The battle was far from over.

I glanced at Aayu, her ethereal form radiating concern and empathy. Despite being a soul, she still felt deeply connected to me. Seeing me covered in blood, she had lost all hope, blaming herself for putting me in this situation. Unaware of my plan, she thought I was merely sacrificing myself.

But I had been waiting for the perfect moment to strike. As the skin walker closed in for the final blow, I saw my chance. With a swift motion, I pulled the dagger, aiming for his head, just as the priest had instructed. The skin walker's superhuman reflexes kicked in, and he swayed back, avoiding the fatal blow. However, the dagger still found its mark, lodging deep in his chest.

The skin walker's eyes widened In agony as he stumbled backward, the dagger's holy power coursing through his body. Though it wasn't enough to kill him, it was clear that he was severely weakened. I knew I had to act fast, or risk losing the upper hand.

Aayu's voice echoed in my mind, "Vaasu, please... be careful." Her concern only strengthened my resolve. I would end this, no matter the cost.

28

Desperate Measures: The Pendant

I knew I had to act swiftly, as the skin walker struggled to escape, his strength waning. As I tried to pull back the dagger for the final blow, he spotted the pendant on the ground. A cunning glint flashed in his eyes, and he realized the pendant alone couldn't harm him. With a sudden burst of speed, he transformed into a black mist and darted into the pendant, seeking refuge and time to recover.

The skin walker thought he had found a safe haven, believing I had no means to extract him from the pendant. But, unbeknownst to him, his desperation had led to a critical mistake. The holy dagger and white ash had weakened him more than he realized.

As the black mist disappeared into the pendant, I smiled grimly. The skin walker had walked right into my trap. I knew the pendant's secret, and now, I had him right where I wanted him.

I gazed at the pendant, now containing the skin walker's misty form. I knew its secret: it could seal dark energies within its confines. With the skin walker's weakened state, he wouldn't be able to escape. He wouldn't die, but he would be trapped for life, a prisoner of the pendant's power.

Aayu's voice was laced with surprise, "Vaasu, why did he go inside the pendant? Won't he come out again?" I took a deep breath, explaining my plan, "I knew the pendant's power, Aayu. It was my Plan B, in case I died in battle. I would wound him, and then trap him in the pendant, saving the village and the souls."

Aayu's eyes widened in understanding, "You planned this all along?" I nodded, "I had to be prepared for any outcome. The pendant was our only hope to contain him, if all else failed." Aayu's gaze fell upon the pendant, now a prison for the skin walker's dark essence. "It's over," she whispered, a mix of relief and awe in her voice.

I smiled grimly, "It's finally over." The skin walker's malevolent presence would no longer threaten our world. The village and the souls were safe, thanks to the pendant's power and my willingness to risk everything.

29

Freedom and Reunion

As the mist surrounding the cursed village began to fade, the villagers slowly returned to their senses. The village, once trapped in a supernatural realm, was finally back in the real world. The captive souls, now free, began to disappear into the afterlife, finally at peace.

I felt my strength waning, my vision blurring. I tried to stay awake, but my body betrayed me. I fell to the ground, unconscious.

When I came to, I found myself in a bed, surrounded by the familiar faces of the villagers, Aayu, and an old doctor. The room was dimly lit, and I was covered in bandages. My wounds had been treated, and I could feel a sense of relief wash over me.

Aayu's eyes, brimming with tears of joy, locked onto mine. She had been waiting anxiously for me to awaken. The villagers smiled, their faces etched with gratitude. The old doctor nodded, his eyes twinkling with warmth.

I tried to speak, but my voice was hoarse. Aayu rushed to my side, helping me sit up, I felt a sense of peace settle over me. We had done it. We had broken the curse and freed the village.

The villagers began to share stories of their experiences, of the mist and the supernatural entities. Aayu held my hand, her grip tight, as if she'd never let me go again. I smiled, feeling a sense of belonging, of being home.

As I gazed at Aayu, I noticed two other souls standing beside her. I instinctively knew they were her parents. They approached me, their eyes filled with gratitude, and thanked me for my bravery. They explained that all the captive souls had moved on to the afterlife, but Aayu had chosen to stay behind, wanting to see me one last time.

Aayu's parents told me that they, too, had wanted to express their thanks in person. Aayu held my hand, her touch surprisingly real. I commented on it, saying it was the second time I'd experienced her touch as real. Aayu asked, "Second time? When was the first, Vaasu?"

I smiled mischievously, "The first time was when you slapped me." The room erupted in laughter, easing the tension. Aayu apologized, explaining that she had only done it to test my resolve and courage. She smiled, "And I was right to choose you."

The atmosphere lightened, and I felt a sense of warmth and connection with Aayu and her parents. I realized that our journey had created an unbreakable bond between us. Aayu's parents began to fade away, their mission accomplished. They bid us farewell, leaving Aayu and me alone once more.

Aayu's gaze locked onto mine, her eyes shining with a deep affection. I knew that our connection went beyond the physical realm. We had transcended into something more profound, something that would last an eternity.

30

The Bittersweet Goodbye

A sudden realization struck me, and I began searching for the pendant and dagger. The villagers' chief noticed my distress and approached me, "Don't worry, boy, here's what you're looking for." He handed me the pendant and dagger, and I felt a sense of relief wash over me.

Aayu's eyes widened as she gazed at the pendant, her expression uneasy. "What are you going to do with it, Vaasu?" she asked, her voice laced with concern.

I smiled reassuringly, "I'll keep it safe with me. It's safer this way, since I have the holy dagger and white ash." I examined the pendant, surprised to see that its broken chain had been repaired. The chief smiled, "We fixed it for you".

I thanked him, feeling a sense of gratitude. As I put the pendant back around my neck, I felt a sense of purpose. The pendant, once a tool for defeating the skin walker, had become a symbol of my responsibility. I vowed to keep it safe, using its power for good.

Aayu's eyes never left mine, her gaze filled with trust and admiration. I knew that our journey had changed us both, forging an unbreakable bond between us. Together, we would face whatever challenges lay ahead, armed with the power of the pendant and our unwavering determination.

As we stood there, Aayu's eyes locked onto mine, and I knew that our time together was drawing to a close. She had to leave, to continue her journey into the afterlife. I tried to hold back my emotions, but they threatened to overwhelm me.

Aayu's voice was barely above a whisper, "Can you stand, Vaasu?" I nodded, despite my wounds, and she asked me to stand. I couldn't deny her request. As I stood, she wrapped her astral form around me, hugging me tightly.

"Thank you, Vaasu," she whispered, her voice trembling. "I'm so grateful to have found a friend like you. I wish I was alive, so I didn't have to leave you." Her words pierced my heart, and I felt a lump form in my throat.

As she hugged me, something miraculous happened. My minor wounds began to heal, the pain subsiding. Aayu smiled, "That's the most I can do for you, Vaasu. It's my thanks to you."

Slowly, her soul began to fade away, her grip on me loosening. I held her tight, cherishing the moment, as the villagers looked on, tears streaming down their faces. Aayu's astral form disappeared, leaving me standing alone, my heart heavy with grief.

The villagers approached me, their faces etched with sadness. They had witnessed our bittersweet goodbye, and it had touched their hearts. I stood there, trying to come to terms with Aayu's departure, knowing that she was finally at peace, but also knowing that I would miss her dearly.

31

The Journey Home

I glanced down at my hand, the wound still present, a reminder of the battle. Though Aayu's hug had healed my minor wounds, this one required more time to mend. Yet, thanks to her, I could walk again, my strength returning.

The villagers, still grateful, requested my presence for a longer period. They offered me gifts, food, and shelter, eager to show their appreciation. I smiled humbly, declining their offers. "My family will be worried about me," I explained. "I must return home."

"Only three days have passed in the real world," the villagers said, "because this time, you defeated the skin walker." I nodded, understanding the significance of our victory.

With a heavy heart, I bid farewell to the villagers, thanking them for their kindness. I began my journey home, the pendant still around my neck, a symbol of my incredible journey. As I walked, I reflected on my experiences, the friends I had made, and the lessons I had learned.

The familiar landscape of my city came into view, and I quickened my pace, eager to reunite with my family. Little did I know, my adventure was far from over. The pendant's power still lingered, and I sensed that my life was about to change in ways I couldn't yet imagine.

As I entered my home, I was met with a familiar scene. My parents, worried and concerned, bombarded me with questions. "Where have you been? What happened to you?" They gasped at the sight of my wounds, their expressions a mix of fear and relief.

But this time, their concern turned to scolding. "We have to keep an eye on you! You don't know how worried we were. Explain everything to us! You came back wounded this time!" I knew I had to lie, unable to reveal the truth about the skin walker and the supernatural world I had encountered.

"I was in a road accident," I said, trying to sound convincing. "I was admitted to a hospital far away. That's why I couldn't contact you." I knew it was a weak excuse, but I had to protect them from the truth.

It was hard to convince them, but eventually, they believed my story. They lectured me about being more careful and responsible, but deep down, I knew they were just relieved to have me back home safe. I felt a pang of guilt for lying to them, but I knew it was necessary to keep them safe from the dangers I had faced.

32

The Pendant's Haunting

That night, as I lay in bed, I started hearing voices emanating from the pendant. The screams and curses sent shivers down my spine. "Let me out!" the voices growled, their malevolent presence suffocating. Every time the voices grew louder, I sprinkled white ash on the pendant, silencing them temporarily.

Days turned into weeks, and I returned to my usual routine, but the pendant's haunting continued. The curses and screams became a constant companion, a reminder of the evil I had trapped. Only I could hear the voices, a burden I carried alone.

But I didn't want to get rid of the pendant. I had grown accustomed to the screams and curses, and I could easily ignore them. This seemed to irritate the trapped entity even more, but I knew it was powerless to harm me. I wore the pendant as a reminder of the responsibility I had taken on – to keep the evil entity contained, to prevent it from harming others. It was a weight I carried, a constant reminder of the danger that lurked within.

The trapped skinwalker soon realized that its curses and threats had no effect on me. So, it changed its tactic, attempting to lure me with offers of power, money, fame, and otherworldly things. But I saw through its schemes and ignored them, even making light of its attempts.

"You're offering me all these things?" I said with a chuckle. "Do you even have a towel in there? How can I trust your promises when you can't even provide a simple towel?"

The skinwalker's responses grew more agitated, its voice rising in anger. But I just laughed, knowing that I had the upper hand. I had trapped it, and it was powerless to harm me.

"Keep trying," I said, taunting it. "Maybe someday you'll come up with an offer that's actually tempting. But until then, I'll just keep ignoring you."

The skinwalker's rage grew, but I just smiled, knowing that I had won this battle of wills. I would continue to wear the pendant, keeping the evil entity contained, and it would continue to try and fail to tempt me. It was a game we played, one that I was determined to win.

33

Custodian Of The Evil

One day I stepped out of the bath, relaxed and refreshed, only to be met with a sight that made my heart skip a beat. My mom held the pendant, admiring its beauty, and asked, "Vaasu, this is a really beautiful pendant. Where did you find it? Can I keep it for myself?"

In that moment, I was flooded with memories of the adversities I faced and the dangers locked inside the pendant. The skinwalker's evil presence, the cursed village, and the countless nights of terror all came rushing back. I panicked, my mind racing with the thought of my mom succumbing to the pendant's dark influence.

I rushed to her, snatching the pendant from her hand, and shouted, "No, you can't have it!" My mom looked taken aback, hurt by my sudden outburst. I realized too late that I had overreacted, but the fear of losing her to the pendant's evil had consumed me.

I took a deep breath, apologizing for my rudeness. "I'm sorry, Mom. This pendant... it's a gift from a close friend. That's why I can't give it to you." I forced a smile, promising to buy her a more beautiful one, and she smiled, unaware of the danger that had just passed.

That day, I decided to keep the pendant with me always, no matter the situation. I couldn't risk losing my loved ones to its evil influence. The skinwalker's whispers had grown fainter, but I knew it was still waiting, patiently, for its chance to strike.

I had won the battle, but the war was far from over. I would carry the pendant, and its secrets, with me forever, always vigilant, always ready to protect those I loved.

www.ingramcontent.com/pod-product-compliance
Lightning Source LLC
La Vergne TN
LVHW041230150826
845673LV00008B/2336